SMALL CEREMONIES

Small Ceremonies

A short story about the small lives and moments we too often overlook~

GINGER ROSS BREGGIN

Lake Edge Press

CONTENTS

To my beloved husband of thirty-six years.
God bless the broken road....

~ 1 ~

The sun was just beginning to lighten the edges of the eastern horizon when he awoke. Slowly pushing the covers off his body, he rose from the bed and went into the bathroom to relieve himself.

"Not Sunday yet," he muttered as he quickly ran cold water from the chipped sink over his knurled hands, sucking in his breath from the pain this caused his arthritis. He knew he didn't have to bathe except for Sundays. Shutting off the water, he quickly left without looking into the mirror or drying his hands. But as he walked into the kitchen he absently raised his fingers to his forehead, smoothing the ragged red scar over his right eye.

He could hear the birds calling him through the open kitchen window as he opened the old refrigerator and pulled out a half can of baked beans left over from the night before. The spoon he had used had been left in the can and he grasped it now, shoveling the beans into his mouth and swallowing almost without chewing. Beans were good. They didn't hurt his gums and they didn't cost a lot. A body cold eat beans and feel full for hours.

The red birds were flitting around in the bushes behind the house, and the grey bird who always sat on his fence post singing the songs of others had taken position and was talking to the morning. It was time to get outdoors.

"Pa said ya have to get out before the sun to find the caps" he whispered to himself as he squinted through the cracked kitchen window at the lightening dawn. He dropped the empty can onto the nicked wooden table and the spoon clattered as the can fell over and slowly rolled across the tilted surface.

He wasn't there to catch it when it fell off the table. It was time to find the caps.

Outside, he sniffed the dew-laden dawn and gimped over to his first rack of caps.

As the sun crested the trees it glinted off the shiny chrome, causing him to squint. Hubcaps lined the dozen racks in neat rows, filling his front and side yard. Some were small and mostly solid with various logos displayed in the center. Others were elaborate spoke and chrome affairs. His favorite had spokes that were fashioned from heavy chain. He never had figured out how they made the chain stiff enough even though once he had spent an afternoon examining the connecting points of the links for glue or solder.

Looked like no one had come by and messed with his caps. Least not last night. For a spell now they had been undisturbed, but earlier, someone had been swiping a couple a night. Once he had sat up until the moon moved almost all the way across the sky, trying to catch the thief. But he was a sly one, like the old coon that got into his garbage. Every time you looked for him he made himself scarce.

Suddenly aware of the growing warmth of the sun on his head, he noticed his shadow growing. He grimaced and glanced at the sky, muttering "early bird, early bird—gets the cap, they say" as he looked at the blue expanse above him. Almost flinching, he whispered, "Papa mad? I'll be good now."

Ignoring the pain in his knees and ankles, he walked out to the road and headed west down Route 29. As he moved along, limping slightly, he scanned the right shoulder and weed-choked drainage ditch for hubcaps. Only way to find 'em was to walk. On a good day, he could find two or three. The bad days happened if his legs gave out or his heart started up so fierce he thought it might fly out of his chest.

Stones suddenly spattered him as a 1972 Chevy sped by, fishtailing as it swerved and throwing gravel.

"Hey! Hubcap man! Made your fortune yet?" Laughter hovered around him long after the stones had fallen to the ground.

"Stupid kids," he mumbled, and kicked a rusty can out of his path. Every generation seemed to breed a few that decided the best fun of all was to laugh at him. Once, they did more than laugh—they came by and took all his hubcaps down one night. He'd been sick then with fever or he would have heard'em. Took him three days to locate the caps, piled in the woods a mile from his place with leaves over them. If he didn't know the woods so well, he would've never seen them. Took even longer to get them home, since his old Ford hadn't worked since '83.

Now they'd gone and got his heart going again. He wouldn't make it to the bridge today before he had to turn around.

But maybe his mother was watching him that morning, because he found four hubcaps in the next two miles, and was able to go home early without upsetting Pa.

$$\sim\ 2\ \sim$$

That evening he sat on his back porch in the battered cane rocker. It worked better since he had found an old piece of plywood to place over the shredded seat. His eyes wandered over his back yard and along the edge of the woods, looking for that coon, and watching the red birds seeking their dusk meal. The air was filled with their cheeping, little pipping sounds that floated through the hazy warmth. The mulberry bushes seemed to draw them as well as the others who came for fruit in the summer. And sometimes, when the winters were fierce and food scarce, he had seen deer venturing out of the woods to eat the lower branches.

His stomach was full of vienna sausage and he had fixed some dandelion greens to go with it that night. Now, he watched the stars come out as the last of the sunset faded to violet and purple.

He felt around on the floor beside him for his papers and can of tobacco and settled the contents in his lap. Not looking, his hands laid a single sheet on his knee and pulled the exact amount of shredded tobacco he needed from the can. He could roll cigarettes in the dark when he needed to. Smoothing the paper, arranging the brown, moist shred down the length of the fragile sheet, he deftly coiled the paper and licked the loose edge to secure it. The plastic Bic lighter he'd found by the road the other day was sitting next to the can and he took it now and shook it, since it was getting low on fluid.

Once lit, he held the cigarette between his thumb and first finger and inhaled. The gossamer trails of smoke drifted up around his face, making the deep lines around his eyes even deeper when he squinted. But it sure did keep away the mosquitoes. It was what he looked forward to all day—the increasing heaviness in his limbs that contrasted with the lightness in his head when he smoked. It was the one good thing his Pa did teach him—but he never let him smoke 'til after sunset. Now he always made sure the sun was below the trees when he smoked, 'cause Pa watched.

Once he had snuck the can and papers out into the woods after returning from his morning hubcap walk. Papa had found him there, laying on his back and smoking his third cigarette.

He hadn't even waited until they got home to beat him. Grabbed a branch big as his wrist and swung it upside his head. When he came to, there was blood in his eyes and for a minute he thought he was blinded. In those days, he would have been glad, cause then he wouldn't have seen hubcaps anymore and could have stayed at home with his mother.

"You get up, boy," his pa had hollered, raising the branch again.

"I can't see! Pa, don't!" he cried as he felt his arm gripped and he was yanked to his feet.

"Jes a little blood—you can see, now walk," Pa answered, and for good measure, kicked him in the direction of home.

But he couldn't see, hardly, and the blood flowed down his face, leaving blooming splotches of scarlet on the green undergrowth. The old log was partially obscured by some poison ivy and he fell over it, hitting the ground with a thump and scraping his shins on the log.

"Get up, get up, get up," his father raged, and the branch came down again and again on his back, his head. He turned, beseeching his father to stop, and the branch caught him in the mouth. Four teeth suddenly filled his throat, and more blood, until he turned over again, retching and spitting out teeth as he curled into a ball on the ground absorbing the blows.

He could barely think, and the fear took him over as he cried, screaming, "I'm sorry, Pa, I'm sorry!"

Pa stalked off, throwing the branch into the woods, and left him to make his own way.

He couldn't rightly remember how old he'd been then—maybe ten or so—no hair on his body yet, anyway.

His Mama had run out screaming when he emerged from the woods. He must have looked like the devil, all covered in red from the blood of his mouth and the gash over his eye. She slipped her arm around his shoulders and he sagged against her breast, bloodying the front of her faded house dress.

"Your dress," he muttered.

"Don't you worry, none. Let's get you to the porch," she said.

"You want to kill him?" she shouted to his father. "You never did want him but now that he's here, you want to kill him?" She settled him onto the sofa that used to be on the back porch and ran over to where his pa stood. Her hands balled into fists, she raised them and pummeled his chest.

"All we've been through and now this! What'd he do? What could be so bad?" she cried, tears streaming down her face as she beat her fists against him.

"Mama, don't!" he called, fighting veils of darkness that seemed to want to enwrap him as he watched his mother pound against his father. Like a gnat on a dog. God, his head hurt.

His father's face darkened and he seemed to grow even larger before he let out a roar and with one swipe of his hand, knocked her clear up against the shed. She shrieked and leapt up once more, but Pa was gone now, swallowed by his rage and he grabbed the pitchfork that stood against the tree and brought it up as she ran at him.

Darkness took him. Ma was gone when he came to, and his pa never spoke of any of it again. There were black stains on the old porch sofa, but Pa said they were from his blood.

The next day he took the sofa to the dump. Darned if he didn't clean forget about it until after Pa died, and then, little by little, it had come back. Sometimes, now, it came at night and he would lay cringing in bed as awoke with tear-stained cheeks to find himself crying for his mother. A man his age...but he didn't feel old; still felt like a boy. Scared of his Pa and missing his mother.

The next morning he decided to cut over to the side road that led to Brandy Station. It was potholed now, and sometimes he got lucky on that stretch. Empty of general traffic, the kids used it as a lover's lane at night and he could see the litter of condoms and Miller beer cans in the weeds.

Once he found a lacy bra and pair of red panties hanging from a tree limb. Remembering this has caused him to become suddenly embarrassed, standing alone on the deserted road. He was glad the kids used this road, though, because when they drove through they usually sped and lost a lot of caps hitting the bumps.

Clouds were thickening overhead like curdled milk as he hurried up the hill, two hubcaps under his arm. His heart pounded and he felt wobbly and light-headed, but he needed at least one more cap.

~ 3 ~

She was in the meadow behind some blackberry bushes watching him as he ascended the hill. His arms were long and hairy and his face looked like a kiwi it was so tanned and stubbly. A puckery scar ran across his forehead, and he was missing his front teeth. Under his arm he carried some hubcaps, and his overalls flapped around his ankles as he walked.

She drew back a little further, afraid he might see her, but he was staring at the ground and she could see sweat running down his face, even though it was cloudy and a wind was picking up.

Then he fell. It was a steep hill, but she never imagined a person could fall backwards like that, straight back, like he was falling into bed. She heard the crack of his head hitting the asphalt, and leapt up, alert as a doe.

He wasn't moving. Was he even breathing? What if a car came-- he'd be run over and killed for sure if he wasn't dead already. Well, he wasn't going to hurt her now.

She wanted to be a doctor someday. Liked medicine so much that she had bought an old edition of *Ship Captain's Guide To Emergency Medicine* at the library sale last year for two dollars. Most evenings she studied it, making up stories about injuries and quizzing herself on what to do for the patient.

Then one day she found a hurt raccoon that looked like it had a leg caught in a trap and chewed it off. It was dazed and laying in the sun, so close to death that when she approached it didn't even

8

move, though its eyes were still open. Flies had gathered on the stump.

She wrapped the raccoon in her sweater and took it home, doctoring it in a box she put in the barn until it started to heal. Eventually, she let it go, but it had lived ever since in her back woods, and she still took it food almost every day. Since then she had cared for other wild things--two squirrels, a wild rabbit, an injured mourning dove, three sparrows, and one deer.

Now it looked like she had her first human patient.

~ 4 ~

"Don't move him," she muttered as she bent over, looking at his face. He looked mustard yellow--pale under his tan, and seemed to be barely breathing. But a car could come at any time, and they were only twenty feet from the crest of the hill. Deciding that he probably hadn't broken his neck from the fall, she grabbed his over-all straps and pulled. He didn't budge.

"Come on" she cried, and then his body slid and she dragged him, down the hill toward the shoulder. Undoing her sweatshirt from around her waist, she gently placed it beneath his head. He moaned.

"Mister, can you hear me, Mister?"

He slowly opened his eyes, and saw three faces in front of him. Long dark hair was caught back in a kerchief framing either side of each face, and her eyes were worried and tender-looking.

"Mother?"

"No, I'm not your mother. I'm Paris. You fell."

"Can't see right. Mama? Pa! What did you do to Mama!" he wailed and suddenly struggled to get up.

She grabbed his shoulders, pushing him back and saying "Easy, easy now. You fell and hurt yourself. Rest a bit before you try to get up. Breathe slow and easy now."

He felt her hands, firm yet gentling, and sunk back against the sweater. Swallowing hard several times, he tried to calm his breath-ing, and found that it did help. The clouds overhead began looking like regular clouds again, and when he turned to look at Paris, he noticed she was a little wisp of a thing, mostly girl, with just a hint of woman peeping through.

"What happened?" he asked.

"I was picking blackberries behind that bush and saw you coming," she replied, pointing toward a thick stand of green at the peak of the hill. "You were climbing this hill, real slowly, and sweating. Then you just fell over—backwards! I heard you hit your head from where I was standing."

"My head hurts," he said, "I need to go home."

"You'd better not go anywhere yet. You must have been mighty dizzy or something to fall like that. Best to rest a bit," as she spoke, she touched his forehead, his shoulder, gentling him wordlessly. He hadn't been touched like this since his mother disappeared. Her eyes, as green as a spring morning, looked steadily at him as she talked.

"You hit real hard and you're bleeding. Can you raise your head a little so I can see?" She slid one hand under his neck to support his head. If felt cool and firm against his skin.

"That gash is bleeding bad--I need to compress it." She spoke low and quiet in her throat, no alarm, no emergency, and he felt his body relax further.

"Roll on your side a bit, that's good. I'm going to bandage you up a little."

He heard fabric tearing and then a firm pressure on the back of his head. She took off her kerchief and tied it, Indian style, around the bandage to hold it in place and apply pressure.

Then she rolled him back on his back.

"Lay there a bit while the bleeding stops. I'd go get help but I'm not sure you'd stay put, and if you don't for a while, you'll fall again. It's more than two miles to the first house with a phone."

"Where'd you get bandages?" he mumbled.

"My undershirt--clean this morning. Now hush and rest."

He felt so strange around her--not afraid like he was with his customers. They were always grown men or teen-aged boys with eyes that seemed to mock him. The men reminded him of his Pa, with thick wrists and hair everywhere--harsh eyes that seemed to absorb everything and give nothing back. But this girl was different--she did remind him of his mother--the only woman he'd known well. He'd had teachers sometimes until Ma went away, then Pa had stopped sending him to school.

"What'd ya need to know to find hubcaps?" Pa would ask.

Besides, since Ma went away he stopped feeling smart, and suddenly, nothing much seemed to matter anyway. He figured hubcaps was all he was good for.

Then he remembered he'd been carrying hubcaps when he fell.

"My hubcaps!" He struggled to rise. "Pa'll be so mad if I forget 'em."

"Easy!" she commanded, placing that little hand on his shoulder again. "I'll fetch them for you if you'll be still."

He obeyed and watched her as she sprang to her feet and walked toward the shoulder of the road. Wading into the tall grasses and pokeweed patches, she soon emerged with the caps. Her long hair swung free around her face, reflecting almost as much sun as the chrome. Then she smiled at him as she returned. He felt as though he'd been blessed.

"Here you go, good as new," she said, and laid the caps by his side.

He fingered the edges of the caps, reassured by their solidness.

"What do you do with them, anyway?" she asked.

"I sell 'em. Have a whole bunch at home. Used to be able to count them when I was little, but something happened to my brain. I can't count much past ten anymore." He felt a slow heat rise in his face as soon as he said this, realizing that, somehow, this was a failing. He suddenly didn't want her to see him that way.

"That's OK. Sounds like you do alright, collecting hubcaps. Do you like it?" Her eyes looked at him directly, reminding him of a Christmas tree ornament he had found one year.

"Actually, Ma'am, I don't know that I do--but my Pa would be so mad if I ever stopped that I just can't. He's watch'n, ya know." Despite the slenderness of her body and her youth, he was suddenly aware of her femaleness, and found the only form of address he had ever used with women springing from his lips.

"What are you calling me Ma'am for? I'm only thirteen!" and she giggled--but it was a laugh of pleasure and seemed not to be aimed at him at all, but at her youth.

"So what should I call you?"

"Paris. My name is Paris, after the city my mother always wanted to visit. Maybe some day she still will. It's a strange name around here, but I don't mind it. Nice name for a doctor someday, and that's what I'm going to be. That's how I knew to put a compress on your head."

He felt the bandage. It seemed to be working and felt dry. No blood came away on his fingers. "Looks like you know your stuff," he replied. "Lucky for me."

"Yes. Now how are you feeling? Dizzy? Seeing double? How many fingers am I holding up?" She produced three fingers, and he counted them off, correctly.

"OK, you're doing better," she pronounced. "Now, can you sit here for about half an hour while I run to get help? The closest phone is about two miles up the road. Oh, and what's your name?"

"Sit here? I can't do that--Pa will be mad. I've gotta get these caps home!" As he spoke, he struggled to get up and this time brushed off her hands. "My name's Cap--short for Hubcap--that's what everybody calls me, since I was a kid."

"Cap? OK. But listen, you can't move, yet. You could fall again."

"Don't matter. Pa'll be mad. Customers come afternoons. Got caps to clean." He bent stiffly, trying to gather the hubcaps she had retrieved earlier.

"I'll get those," she said quickly, scooping them up from the ground. "If you won't let me go for help, at least let me walk you to hour house--and I don't mind carrying your hubcaps for you." This guy wasn't going to stay put if she went for help, and he could end up staggering in front of a car when he got onto Route 29--then he'd really be a goner. Besides, if she could walk him home, maybe he'd let her clean that wound. It was embedded with gravel and needed disinfecting. Something about him wasn't right--he was the meekest man she'd ever met, so it wasn't danger she felt.

His eyes looked like the eyes of the squirrels she had doctored--fearful and trusting all at once, like they sensed her good intentions but still fought their instincts to flee.

~ 5 ~

The walk to his house took less time than she expected. He really was pretty strong under all that scrawniness. Once she asked him a question that had been bothering her.

"How old are you, Cap?"

"Don't know, anymore," he answered. "But I remember Pa saying I would have gone to fight in World War II if I wasn't so dumb. Must make me pretty old now."

"And your Pa is still alive? He must be really old," she replied, reaching the source of her confusion.

"Naw, Pa died. He was chopping wood one morning when I came back from getting caps. Sweatin' and muttering, with that wild look in his eyes. Maybe he'd been drinkin' the moonshine he used to make. Saw me coming with just two caps and the sun real high and figured I'd been bad again. Started raving and came at me with the ax."

"What happened?" she asked, shocked.

"He tried to ax me. Missed, and fell." Cap was quiet a moment as they walked. Paris's eyes never left his face as they walked together, but she said nothing.

"Pa looked up once. Lifted his face out of the dirt. Said 'I'm watchin' ya, boy.' Never got up again."

"He died?"

"Yup. Stiffened up, too."

"What happened to the body?"

"Pa said, if ever the police heard me talkin', I'd be locked up forever. No more smokes. No more birds or mulberry bushes. They hurt ya bad in them places. So I put him in the old well. Dried up years ago. Needed to be filled in, anyway."

Paris stumbled. Caught herself. A body in a well? This old witless man living alone?

"How do you take care of yourself?"

"Get a check every month. Social Security. Cash it at Blackwell's down the road a piece. Buy my food there and eat greens and berries. Sometimes, I catch a rabbit, usin' snares--not guns. Then I sell a few caps now and then. I get by."

She glanced up and saw they had reached his house. Good thing. The rain was just starting and thunder rumbled. The first few drops hit the dust leaving pockmarks in the dirt path as they hurried to the door. Surrounding the house were row upon row of hubcaps and as they reached the open porch she heard the melodic pings of droplets striking metal.

"Caps sing when it rains. Sometimes it sounds like music Ma used to play. Real full and tinkley."

"It's like magic," she breathed, listening as the varied pitches of the caps came together in a sound like a thousand Christmas bells. A bolt of lightning suddenly made her jump.

"Indoors," he said, and led the way.

The interior was closed in and dark and smelled like an old basement. She saw an empty can of Campbell's baked beans under the wooden table with a crusted spoon next to it. For some reason it reminded her of why she was here.

"Do you have any iodine?"

Cap produced a small brown bottle with a faded label from a cupboard.

"Sit here and let me wash your wound," she instructed. Taking off the bandage she had fastened, she used her kerchief to clean the cut.

He sat motionless throughout the ordeal, not even sucking in his breath. His utter quiet brought to mind the rabbit she had doctored. Not a single sign of the pain she must be causing had been visible.

Once the gash was cleaned she painted it with the iodine and tore her shirt further to make a smaller, neater bandage.

"There," she said, announcing the completion of her task and her pleasure in how they had both done.

He turned to her and with sudden dignity, said "Thank you."

She smiled.

"Something's been bothering me," she said. "How come you keep thinking your pa is going to be mad at you?"

Cap sat back. This was a question that had never occurred to him. "He said he'd be watchin'. Sometimes, things don't go right. I figure Pa's mad at me cause he's been watchin'."

"But he's dead."

"Yup. Still watchin' though, from the sky, and from the well."

She thought about this and about this old man who sat before her, still fearing his father after all those years. He was barely getting by--probably not eating right, and maybe he needed a doctor. Something made him fall today. It might be his heart.

"You ought to let someone help you, y'know. Maybe you'd be happier in a home or someplace where there are other people."

Cap leapt up from his chair. The crash as it hit the floor reverberated in the kitchen.

"Don't you start telling' me what I should do. I get by here just fine all on my own. Don't need no body's charity." His hands trembled and he placed them on the table to steady himself, but his eyes seemed to shoot sparks.

"I don't need people meddlin' in my business," he declared and turned away.

The silence stretched out like the taffy she'd pulled last week as she looked at his rigid back and thought about what he'd said.

It came to her in a flash, then. Her struggle with that deer. The whites of its eyes and its fight to escape the confines of the barn. It hadn't eaten anything for the three days she kept it. Long enough to seal up its wound but not long enough to watch it heal.

The last day she had sat, looking at the doe as it paced from door to door in the barn, sniffing deeply at the fresh fall air through the cracks. In just three days its coat had lost much of its sheen and its eyes had grown dull.

She knew if she didn't let it go and be the wild spirit it was, that it would die. With a sigh she had walked to the door and opened it. The doe had taken two tentative steps out of the barn and turned to look over her shoulder at Paris.

"Go on--it's what you wanted!" she cried, fighting tears.

Before her eyes then it transformed into the graceful, native creature it was meant to be. Kicking up her heels, the deer had run into the back meadow, bounded over the spring, and disappeared into the woods. Paris had wondered for months what happened to her. She never found a carcass, but most dead wild things don't get found.

Then one clear spring dawn she had awakened early and walked outside. The sun sparkled on the dew and the tender green grass shoots glistened in the morning breeze. In the middle of the meadow, with a fawn at her side, stood the doe. The scar across her shoulder stood out in stark relief against her soft coat as she stood, ears pointed, and looked straight at Paris. Then, in a flash of white tails and hooves, they were gone.

Paris learned about freedom that day and remembered it now as she looked over at this frail old man.

Finally she spoke.

"I'm really sorry. I wouldn't make you go anywhere." He was right; he'd die in a hospital or some other place. But did he have to fear every day?

"What if I told you your pa could never hurt you again?" she asked. The rain drummed steadily now on the cracked kitchen window.

"I couldn't believe you. He's not restin' yet. I never knowed no prayers to say." Caps eyes grew shiny, and he reached up and absently stroked his scar. "Nor for my Ma. They both watch. But Ma never could stand up to Pa."

She thought of the Presbyterian church she went to on Sundays. Cap would be scared of the minister. She remembered the times she went to the Catholic Church in Warren with her friend Mary. Incense and lit candles; chants and kneeling and crossing yourself.

She had candles--a whole collection of them in her room. Her favorites were the squat little votive candles in their small glass containers. When one burned down you just lifted out the little metal square that held the wick and replaced it with another.

"Cap, I know how to pray. I learned it in church. I've been baptized, too, I'm allowed to do this stuff. Want me to do a ceremony for you? You could put your Ma and Pa to rest and give them peace."

His eyes were looking out the cracked kitchen window through the rain at the willow tree on the north side of the property. They had a porcelain glaze and he sat so still she thought he hadn't heard her.

"No one needs to know?" he finally asked.

"Our secret," she assured him.

"How soon?"

"I can come back today."

~ 6 ~

She returned two hours later, wearing a yellow slicker and leaving puddles as she walked into the kitchen.

"You came back," he said.

"Of course. I promised." she replied.

"I've made some tea." He gestured toward the table. "Ain't got no milk, but there's sugar." Two cracked china cups stood side by side next to a tea pot with a hissing lid. The one cup had a garland of violets running along it's rim. The second cup was had a tuliped edge with a hint of remaining gold border. Steam rose from the earthenware pot. An old jelly jar held some sugar.

"Tea! That's perfect. I'll just set my things out."

She removed a box of six scented votive candles and two holders, one fat red candle, three cones of incense, and a Bible, placing them on the table.

"Let's have our tea," she suggested.

He was quiet as they drank. She spoke of the animals she had doctored; how they had responded, how they had healed, and twice, how they had died.

"I like the critters myself," he finally responded. "Been watchin' the red birds for years."

"Cardinals. That's what they're called. Birds can be a lot of company."

"Sure can. So are the rabbits and the squirrels. Fact is, my ma never liked mice, but when I find a nest I watch em, real careful like so as not to scare 'em away. They're as busy as I am. Most pleasure I get these days is watching the critters. They're my neighbors."

She nodded. She understood.

"Where would you like to have your ceremony place?" she asked. "A place you can keep these things? Maybe the spot in the house you like the most?"

"Back porch is my favorite," he answered, and helped her carry the candles and incense outside.

She went back into the kitchen and came out with an old lace runner and the Bible.

"This is going to be the alter, Cap." She laid the dusty plastic milk crate that stood in one corner on its side and draped the lace runner over it. Then she went back to the kitchen for the candles. The rain had stopped but the late afternoon silence was punctuated by an occasional drip that still fell from the porch roof.

"Here are your candles--one for each of your parents. And here is some incense. You set it on a plate, like this. I brought some matches, too, just in case you don't have any. Here, light the candles."

He took the matches and cupping the flame in his gnarled hands, lit the two small candles and the large stubby one.

"The red candle smells like cinnamon and the little pink ones are strawberry. Now, light the incense."

He did that, too, and then they stood back for a minute, silent. The flames from the candles sputtered slightly in the rain-soaked evening breeze and danced against the darkening shadows. Curls of smoke drifted up from the incense cone, filling their heads with the scent of pine and wet woods.

"Can you read this, Cap?" she asked, handing him the Bible. He shook his head. No.

"Hold it in your hands, then. This is God's book. It is holy. When you hold it, God knows you want to talk and he'll come visit you on this porch. Now, let's kneel."

They knelt in front of the alter. The skinny, scarecrow of an old man the wisp of a girl-woman, her hair shining in front of the candlelight. He held the Bible against the scar on his forehead and closed his eyes, inhaling the leather smell of it and feeling its pliability between his hands.

"Dear God," she began. "We are here to pray for Cap's Ma and Pa. Nobody prayed for them before. Cap thinks they are sad and their spirits are here. They lived hard lives, and died hard deaths. Could you bring them home now, to you? They need some rest, and so does Cap. Amen."

"Amen." he echoed.

They continued to kneel, silent. Then, from the backyard, a mockingbird began its evening song, the trills and notes of its voice filling the gathering dusk, drifting through the air like the incense.

Finally, he stirred.

"Maybe Pa's not angry anymore?" he asked.

"He can't be angry if he's resting with God," she replied.

"That's good," he sighed.

~ 7 ~

She visited him once, a month later, and brought him some more votive candles. He had been lighting them each night at dusk, before smoking his cigarettes. The Bible she had given him had curled slightly from the damp of the porch air, but he seemed to cherish it, leaving it between the candles in a place of honor. His wound had healed, leaving one more scar on his well-worn body.

One day she came and found the back door open. The Bible rested between the candles, and a pack of matches lay nearby. His can of tobacco and papers sat next to the old cane rocker. He wasn't in the house, and the door had been open so long that leaves had blown inside. He had to have been gone for days.

Paris found the box of votive candles and took one out. As she lit the three small candles and the large red one, the mockingbird began to sing from the mulberry bush and the air stirred, lifting her hair from her face. She waited until it was almost fully dark, but he was not coming home again.

When she was finished, she gathered up the candles, Bible and incense, wrapping them in the old runner covering the milk carton. She went home and asked her mother to call the sheriff. Then she went to her room where she had created her own small alter. She added the candles and incense, and placed the Bible in a position of honor. The runner was draped across the back, a reminder of him and his story.

They never found his body. Paris figured he must have gone off by himself, like one of her wild creatures, to die, finally at peace.